A
Best
Friend's
Promise

Latoya Carter

NEWMAN SPRINGS PUBLISHING
320 Broad Street
Red Bank, NJ 07701

First originally published by Newman Springs Publishing 2024

ISBN 979-8-89308-614-0 (Paperback)
ISBN 979-8-89308-615-7 (Digital)

Printed in the United States of America

CHAPTER

1

Sunday is here.

"Hello! Can you hear me calling you? Susie, if you do not answer me at this moment—"

"Yes, Mama!"

"Are you up and ready?"

"No!"

"Honey, you know we have to be on the road in two hours. The movers are here, loading all our belongings now."

"Well, don't worry because I am up now," I mumble. I don't want to even move. Ugh!

As I head to the bathroom, I smell something that smells *amazing*. OMG! Mom made my favorite breakfast. Now I'm motivated. I hurry to get ready.

The last thing I do is brush my teeth. I'm all done now.

After running downstairs to the kitchen with the biggest smile on my face, I hug my mom while saying, "I love you, and thank you so much." I sit down and say grace before eating.

Walking back through the house, I make sure everything is packed up. As I go down the hall, I come across a huge crack in the wall.

I hear, "Susie! Come on, honey. It's time to go."

"Okay, here I come."

We are all loaded up and ready to hit the road. Looking out the window, I wave goodbye to the house I've spent my whole life in. I must have dozed off because I woke up to my mom's voice saying, "Honey, get up. We've made it."

I stretch and yawn, nodding my head, saying, "Okay."

Getting out of the car, I look at the new house in shock. It looks good, just not as big as our old house. I guess we don't need too much space anymore. While approaching the front door, I hear a soft meow. Pausing for a moment, I wonder aloud, "Where are you, little kitty?" Right as I say that, here comes a beautiful baby kitten. I pick the kitten up and kindly ask my mom if it's okay to keep it.

With a small grin, she says, "Yes."

As the door opens, I exclaim, "Wow, it's actually gorgeous!"

I walk around to find my room and spot a pool out the kitchen window. "Oh yeah!"

Mom yells for me to come downstairs. As I make it down to the last step, she tells me we will grab something to eat while the movers get the furniture and everything else inside.

We drive around to find a good restaurant in town. It is very hard to decide, but we come across a nice place to eat. During dinner, Mom asks if I am ready to start going to this new school. Like any kid, I'm never ready to start a new school. All of those thoughts run wild in my mind.

"To be honest, Mom, I have no choice but to be ready."

She just looks at me with a huge smile. "I know, honey, this all was sudden."

Looking back at her, I tell her honestly, "As long as we have each other and are both safe, it's okay."

Leaving the restaurant, we head back home. Finally, I can get my room together before going to bed, making sure I'm up and ready for the first day of this new school.

CHAPTER

2

Rooms all together, teeth brushed, and pj's on—there's just one more thing to do before bed. I go to my mom's room.

"Hey, Mom!"

"Hey, honey, my little Susie Q. Hopefully, we can get a good night's rest."

"No worries, Mama, we will."

"Aww, I love you, honey."

"I love you, Mama. Good night!"

"Goodnight!"

Heading back to my room, I hear that soft meow again. Looking down, I see the little kitten purring while rubbing against my leg. I pick her up, whispering, "Do you mind if I call you Kit?" I laugh at myself when I catch myself thinking she's really going to answer back.

The alarm clock buzzes loudly. Oh, how I want to hit Snooze but can't. "Up, up, and away," I say, laughing while getting out of bed. As I finish getting ready, I call for my mom. No answer. Why no answer? Normally, she's yelling for me.

I go to her room and see she's still sleeping. I whisper softly while shaking her, "Mom, time to wake up."

She mumbles, "Just a little while longer."

"Can't do that, Mama. I will be late for school."

Popping up her head, she says, "Oh my gosh, I forgot."

After we arrive at school, Mom takes me to the main office to get registered. I get my schedule, and off to my first class I go. Interestingly, my first three classes are my favorite subjects: history, math, and science. Halfway through the day, it's finally lunchtime. I probably have to sit alone because I haven't made any friends, which is no big deal since it's my first day. I find a table no one is sitting at and sit there. Before I can start eating, I hear a girl's voice asking if she can sit with me. Looking up, I say, "Of course. I don't own the table." I smile and then laugh so she knows it's a joking gesture.

"Thanks," she says, then introduces herself. "Hi, my name is Lynn."

"My name is Susie. Are you new here as well, Lynn?"

She replies by shaking her head side to side.

"Oh, okay."

After lunch, I go to my next class. Walking into the classroom, I see Lynn waving me over to sit by her. I smile, hurry over to the desk, and sit down, thanking her.

"No problem," she says.

Lynn ends up being in all three of my last classes. *How awesome is that?* I think.

On my way back home after school, I say to myself, "This place may not be that bad after all."

I tell my mom how it went at school on the first day. She takes a sigh of relief.

Now it feels like the night can't go by fast enough. Finally, I drift off to sleep.

Morning comes, so I get up early to cook breakfast for Mom. I'm not really a chef, but hey, she'll love it. I'm sure of it.

The table's set. Now I can hear Mom coming down the stairs. She comes around the corner, looks surprised at what I've done, kisses my forehead, and then thanks me.

Knock, knock, knock!

"Huh?" my mom says. "Who might that be?"

"I'll get it," I say as I jump up and start running to answer the door.

"Hey, Susie!" Lynn says.

"Hey, what are you doing here?"

"Wondering if you would like to walk to school this morning."

"Let me ask. Hold on really quick, okay? Mom, can I walk to school?"

"Wait just a second. With who?" my mom asks in kind of a loud but soft, caring voice.

"Oh, I meant to tell you I have a friend. Her name is Lynn. *We* will be late if I don't hurry up, Mama. Please!"

"Okay, honey. Just be very careful."

"I will, thanks."

Walking down the street, we begin to talk about a school dance. Lynn speaks about all the stuff that happens and asks if I want to attend. Of course, I am not really sure about going because I barely know anyone.

We make it to school, and over the intercom, we hear the principal talking about the school dance as well. Tickets will go on sale today until next week, on Friday.

Now lunchtime has come. As Lynn and I sit eating our lunch, she brings up the dance again.

"Okay, listen, I don't mind going as long as you're sure you will be there as well. Plus, I have to ask my mom, then I can give you a for sure answer."

Lynn says, "*Perfect!* I'm sure your mom will let you go. Also, Susie, I'm going to make a promise that I will be there. So you know for sure, I will even have my mom pick you up and take us. Susie, I want you to know that you are my best friend. Since you've arrived at this school, my days are much better. I'm a happier person. I was waiting to give you this best-friend charm, but I think now would be a great time."

As I look at her and grab the gift, I smile big and thank her for being a great friend. I see she has the same one on. Wow! I open it and it reads, "Best." I look at hers, and it reads, "Friend." Now I can't let her down. We have to go to this dance. As the school day comes to an end, I get super excited to get home to ask if I can go.

Walking out of the school building, I see my mom waving for me to come on. Hmmm, interesting. She didn't tell me she was coming to pick me up today. I run to the car and start to open the door for the front seat. I have the biggest smile on my face. My mom, of course, just knows I want something.

Laughing out loud, she asks, "What is it, Susie Q?"

"What do you mean? I...I mean," I stutter, "what makes you think I want something?"

"Honey, I've known you all your life, so when you have that look with that smile, it speaks to me."

"Well, since you know me so well, I do have something to ask you."

"Okay, honey, go ahead."

"So there's a school dance coming up, and I was—"

"*OMG! Yes, Susie, you may go.*"

"*Huh?* Mom, why are you so excited?"

"Because I've worried about you since the sudden move. It just makes me sad to have uprooted you from what you've known to be home your whole life. So to see you adjust so well is all I could—" She gets choked up on her words, and tears start falling down her cheeks.

"Aww, Mama, you know I understand why we had to go so quickly." As I find a napkin to dry her eyes, I say, "Nothing will ever make me put the blame, or any blame, for that matter, on you. Wanting the best for me as well as yourself is absolutely the best decision you could have ever made. Now don't cry, and no worrying. We are going to be just fine."

My mom looks at me with so much love in her eyes. She grabs me, pulls me closer, and hugs me—of course, with a squeeze.

"Okay," I giggle, then say, "I love you, Mama!"

She kisses my forehead and says it back.

"When do you need to purchase your ticket?"

"I have until next Friday. Is it possible to maybe go in there now to get it?"

"Well, we can try. What can it hurt, right?"

"Right!"

So my mom parks the car, and we head back into the school building. We go to the office to see if it is possible to get the tickets now or if I have to wait until tomorrow.

"Hi, Miss Kim!" I say as we walk through the double doors to the main office.

"Well, hello there, little Ms. Susie. What can I help you with?"

"Uh, well, I want to purchase a ticket for the school dance that's coming up."

"Okay! Hold on for just a second while I grab the ticket envelope."

While we wait for her to get back to us, I ask my mom if it would be okay to buy two tickets—one for me and one for my best friend.

She smiles and says, "Sure, whatever you want to do, my sweet daughter."

"Thank you!"

"You are most welcome!"

"Okay! So, Susie, how many would you like to get?"

"Two tickets, please."

"Oh, okay, perfect. That will be a total of $10.50."

"All right, here you go."

"Here are your two tickets. Have a wonderful day."

"Bye!" I wave as we leave the office.

As we head back to the car, my mom notices my Best Friend necklace.

"Oh my, that is beautiful, Susie."

"Thanks! My best friend, Lynn, gave it to me today."

"Well, that's really sweet of her."

"Yes, that's why I bought her a ticket for the dance, to show my appreciation for her being a great friend to me and making me comfortable here at this new school."

"I completely understand," says my mom. "So it was a good thing I picked you up today, huh?"

"Yes, it truly was."

"Susie, we should go to the mall and check out some stores to find you a beautiful dress."

"Really, Mom?"

"Yes, really!"

"Okay, great, let's go."

It takes, like, maybe twenty-five minutes to get to the mall from school. Now we are here. There are so many stores to choose from. My anxiety is through the roof. I'm excited, happy, and worried about what I will find for this dance of mine. Yikes! OMG! Yahoo! Just a little of everything.

"Mom!" I yell, smiling.

She is amazed at the dress in the store display window. "Wow, sweetie, that is it."

"You think so, mom?"

"Yes, indeed, I do. Let's go see if they have your size and a dressing room for you to try it on."

When we walk into the store, a lady greets us, saying, "Welcome in today. If there is anything I can help you with, just give me a holler. My name is Paige."

"Hi!" I say overly loud because I'm so excited.

My mom whispers, "Shush, why so loud, Susie dear?" She apologizes for my behavior, letting Paige know I'm just super excited to get the dress for my school dance.

Paige says, "It's completely understandable. Is there one you already have your eyes set on?"

"Yes! It's the one in the window over there."

"Nice choice. That is a beauty. We actually just got it in today, so I feel it's your lucky day."

"Wow! Okay, so can I try it on?"

"Absolutely! Let me grab it down for you. Also, I'll check the size to let you know just in case you want a certain size or fit."

"Perfect!"

Paige goes over to the place where the dress is. She glances at the size tag and looks back with a big smile. "Okay, ladies, I think this was definitely meant for you."

"What!" I scream, jumping up and down. *Breathe. Just calm down and breathe,* I say in my mind to myself.

"Here you are, little lady, and the dressing room is right over there."

"Okay, thanks so much."

"No problem!"

"Mom, I'll be right back."

"Okay!"

"While walking quickly to the dressing room, I look back and see Paige and my mom talking and laughing. It feels good to see her smile and laugh again. It's amazing how things in life can happen to someone that makes them never look or feel genuinely happy.

Bam!

Ouch… So embarrassing! I was so busy being nosy I just ran into the door of the dressing room. They look at me as I laugh, holding my hand up, saying, "I'm fine, no worries at all." I hurry into the dressing room and close the door quickly.

This fits exactly the way I want. Also, it looks exquisite on me. I feel like a princess; all I need is a crown. Giggling, I do the wave of a beauty queen.

Knock, knock!

"Susie, are you going to let us see?"

"Oh yeah, Mom, here I come."

As I walk out, my mom's eyes get big and fill up with tears. Paige's mouth drops, then she brings it back up with a smile.

I ask, "Well…what do you guys think?"

"Gorgeous," says Paige.

My mom is still in shock. She takes a deep breath and says, "Absolutely stunning. You are growing into a beautiful young lady."

"Thank you both," I say, grinning, feeling myself getting hot because the attention is on me. People in the store are looking at me, talking about how beautiful I look. So this one is it. Now I go to take it off.

When I meet them back at the counter, Paige asks if I have any shoes for this lovely dress I'm getting.

"No, not yet."

"Can I show you guys some that we've just got in today?"

I pause to look up at my mom, waiting for her to answer because I don't know how much I can spend.

"Of course, you can," Mom says.

Paige goes to the back and brings out at least five pairs of stylish, classy, casual shoes.

Must I say, that made it even harder to choose from. All the decisions to make, sheesh. Nevertheless, I find the perfect ones. Now my stomach makes a growling noise.

"Oh my," says my mom. "Are you hungry?"

All the thinking has given me quite the appetite. We thank Paige for her help, and after showing our deepest gratitude, we leave.

CHAPTER

3

We get back to the house, and Mom heads straight to the kitchen to start dinner so we can eat soon and watch a movie before bed.

"Hey there, Kit. How are you, my cute little fuzzy friend? Did you miss me? I've had an amazing day. Still, I missed you for sure. Hope you're up for movie night after dinner."

Kit responds with a meow and lots of purring.

I take it as a yes.

After dinner, I ask Mom what kind of popcorn she would like for our movie. "Extra butter, white cheddar, kettle corn, or caramel?"

Of course, she picks the best: white cheddar.

"What is the movie?"

"*The Notebook*!"
"Okay!"

"It was definitely a tearjerker, Mom. Well, good night."

"Good night, sweetie!"

Morning arrives pretty fast, I must say. Up and ready for my day at school, I am super happy to surprise Lynn with her ticket for the dance. Off to school I go.

To my surprise, I haven't seen Lynn yet, which is very odd because we always meet in front of the school and chat for a while before class. Hmmm, well, I'll see her in third period, I'm sure. I hope all is okay.

It seems like every class is taking forever to be over so I can see her. The bell finally rings for third period. I go straight to class, and as the room fills up, there's no Lynn. This seems so strange. Normally, she would be here by now.

No worries, I'm going to think positively about the situation. She's probably out sick today. I hope she feels better if so.

School is going by really slowly. I feel as if I'm in a never-ending dream. Okay, last class. I feel worried because it's weird that she's not here. All in all, I am sure I'll see her tomorrow. I should have known she wouldn't be here today because she didn't come to walk to school with me this morning, nor was she in our meeting spot.

"Long day today?" Mom says as I walk in the front door.

"Yes, it actually was, and a bit strange."

"Oh, why?"

"Well, Lynn wasn't there today, so I couldn't give her the surprise ticket I got for her for the dance or tell her I can go. I guess I was a little disappointed, that's all."

"Well, my little Susie Q, I am sure she had a good reason not to have been there today. It's only one day."

"I know, Mama. I just had something import-ant to give her and let her know."

"Do you want me to make your favorite meal for dinner?"

"No, Mama, I don't really have an appetite. I'll just go up to my room to do some homework and then go to bed. It'll be an early night for me."

"Well, honey, you have to at least put some food in that tummy of yours."

"I know. Maybe when I get some work done and take a shower, and then my appetite might come. I'm just in my head overthinking, that's all."

"Love you, Susie honey."

"Love you, Mom."

I enter my room, and Kit greets me. Giggling, I say, "You sure do know when to pop up, huh?"

Kit's purring!

"Let's see, what do I want to work on first? Eeny, meeny, miny, moe, catch a tiger by the toe. If it hollers, let it go."

I hear my mom yelling, "Hey Susie!"

"Yes, Mom!"

"I was thinking we get the pool all cleaned up and ready to use for the weekend."

"Seriously? But I have homework."

"It's the weekend. It can wait, can't it? At least until Sunday? I figure that would help keep your mind from worrying about Lynn until you see her on Monday morning, you know?"

With a deep sigh, I answer, "Yeah." But in my mind, I'm hoping she comes over this weekend so I can give her the ticket and see if she's okay. It just doesn't make much sense. It seemed so important to her that we go to the dance.

"So, Mom, do we need to go to the hardware store for some stuff to get started on the pool?"

"Yes, we actually do. Let's go!"

We get a lot of good stuff for cleaning the swimming pool. Back home, we unload the car and head to the backyard.

"Mom, I've never cleaned a pool out. You know that, right?" I laugh out loud as I look at her to see what her response will be.

Smiling, she says, "Honey, I had no clue."

Laughter rings out between us both. This will surely be interesting.

Following the instructions on the package, we begin our journey. So far, everything is going great. Then all we hear is crackling with a loud boom.

"Oh my, here comes the rain." Both of us pause with shocked looks on our faces. I grab my mom and start singing to her. We dance in the rain while singing. *I love my mom so much.* No matter what, she is always here through the good times and the bad times.

Lightning starts to light up the sky.

"Susie, honey, it's time to head in, don't you think?"

"Definitely, Mama."

"Well, doesn't this just rain on our parade. Hehe! Got to get out of these wet clothes."

Upstairs I go. As I walk into my room, I still worry about Lynn. I try to figure out if there were any red flags indicating that something was wrong or going on in her life that she didn't want to tell me because she thought I would judge her or not care.

While thinking of this, my mind drifts back to the day my mom picked me up from my old school. She told me we couldn't go back home and would be staying at a hotel. I insisted we had to go home because my project was due the next day.

She looked at me with such sadness on her face, saying, "Okay, I will go back, but promise me you'll stay in the car while I run in to get it?"

"Mom, why can't we just stay home?"

"Susie! Listen to me. We are not staying. Is that understood?"

By the tone of her voice, I knew I had better agree. "Okay, Mom, understood."

Now we were pulling in the driveway. She told me to lock the doors until she came back out. She ran in. I was looking around and saw my dad's car.

"Oh, Dad's home. Hmm, I wonder why I can't go in. I want to say hi to my dad. But Mom told me to stay in the car and keep the doors locked."

About thirty minutes went by, and Mom hadn't come out yet. I told her exactly where my science project was sitting. Strange! I got out of the car, and as I ran inside, I heard a big bang. As I went up the steps, I saw Mom duck down as if she was dodging something.

I yelled, "Mom!"

She looked up, crying.

The man standing over her turned as he pulled his fist from the wall. He said, "Hey, Susie baby!"

I looked with shock written all over my face.

Mom got up, walked to me fast, and said, "Come on, honey."

We basically ran out the door, forgetting my project and all. We got in the car as the doors shut, and my dad stood in the doorway of our home, looking with such devastation on his face. I looked down to avoid making eye contact with him, thinking, *He's a monster.* That must have been the reason we should not have come back. Bringing Mom and making her go through this made me feel really bad.

"Mom, I am so sorry. I had no clue."

"Honey! Don't worry. I've been hiding this from you for a while now, giving your father chance after chance, but I still get the same results. Time has come for me to make one of the hardest decisions I've had to make, without a doubt, but the most important thing for me is making sure you're safe. No more wishing and hoping he does right."

As we arrived at the hotel, Mom went in. We got to the room, and her phone was ringing nonstop. She didn't answer, of course.

Nothing else was really said after all of this happened. We ate and then fell asleep. I woke up to my mom listening to a voice message. I couldn't hear much, just that he was leaving and that we could come back to the house. By the look on Mom's face, she didn't trust it. She started to dial a number. The voice sounded like Ray. Ray was a cop who was really good friends with Mom and Dad. I think they all went to school together.

She asked him to check on our house to see if there was anyone there.

"Of course, I can. Is everything okay?"

"Yeah and no," said Mom.

"Well, tell me what's going on."

"Right now is not a good time. I have to get Susie to school and see if I need to get the hotel for a few more days."

"Okay! Listen, you get her to school. I'll run by the house to check it out. I'll give you a call then to let you know what's up."

"Perfect! Thank you again."

"No problem."

Mom did manage to get us some clothes packed in a bag, so I was able to get ready for school.

As we headed out, it was nothing but silence inside the car. I wasn't sure if I should say anything, honestly. When we arrived at school, I told Mom I loved her.

"Love you, Susie Q. I'll be here to pick you up, okay?"

"Yes, okay, Mom."

"Oh, also, Susie, I already explained to your teacher about you not having your project today. She said it'll be okay. Just bring it in next week."

"Wow! Okay, thanks."

"Have a good day, honey."

"See you later, Mama."

"Susie. Susie. Susie?"

"Huh? What? Yes?" I say, opening my eyes and seeing Mom standing with a candle.

"You okay, sweetheart?"

"Yes, I must have dozed off or something."

"Well, I brought you a candle because the power has gone out. I didn't want you to be in the dark."

"Oh, thank you, Mom. You're amazing!"

"I try," she says.

"No lights means no TV. How about we tell scary stories?" I laugh creepily after saying it.

Mom looks at me while jumping on the bed, saying, "Sure. But first, we have to build our tent."

"Yes, Mama, perfect."

I run to the hall closet and open it to grab everything we need, from sheets to blankets. Mom grabs pillows and flashlights.

"Where to build the tent, Mom?"

"Let's go in the living room."

As soon as we start our story time, the lights pop on.

"Here, let me go turn them off."

"Really, Mom?"

"Yeah!"

I love how close my mom and I have gotten. Sometimes a person's scars prevent them from being who they really are.

After my story, both of us start getting sleepy. We decide to sleep in the tent.

Morning comes, and we both must have been sleeping hard because we wake up to a loud, repeated knock. I jump up, thinking Lynn has come over. When I get to the door, it's some guys.

"Oh, honey, it's the pool cleaners. I figured we'd better call for backup." She giggles and says, "Come on in. Let me show you guys the pool area."

My head drops. I walk slowly back into the living room to clean up our tent stuff.

4

Well, I got all my work done. The swimming pool is ready for swimming. School is here, and I'm ready to get there to see if there is any sign of Lynn. In front of the school? Nope, no Lynn. Going from one class to another, I hope to at least run into her in the halls. Still nothing. When third period comes, I'm definitely asking the teacher. This just seems weird, and I'm very concerned and confused.

The bell rings, and I go straight to third period without stopping by my locker or anything.

"Hey, Ms. Daniels."

"Well, hello, Susan. What's up?"

"I need to ask you a question."

"Sure! What is it?"

"Well, last week my friend Lynn didn't come to class."

Someone begins to call Ms. Daniels. She tells me to hold on one second and walks to see who's calling her name. Now students are rolling into class. As she walks back in, the bell rings. I look at her, shake my head, and go to my seat. Looking at Lynn's seat, I see she's still not here.

Class is over, and as I begin to walk out, Ms. Daniels says, "Susan."

"Yes?"

"Did you still have something you wanted to ask me about?"

"Just wondering about—"

Before I can get anything else out, the fire alarm goes off.

"Oh my, let's hurry out of here."

Over the loudspeaker, we hear, "Everyone outside. Single-file lines out to the ball field ASAP."

Hurrying out of the school, Ms. Daniels says, "I'm not sure which Lynn you are talking about. Come to me tomorrow with a last name, and I can better help you."

"Okay, thanks."

Reaching the destination, we stand until they get us counted so we can go to lunch.

"Excuse me!" someone says.

"Oh, sorry, didn't mean to be in the way."

Giggling, he says, "No, you're not in the way at all."

"Oh, okay, good." Smiling, I turn back around.

"Well, my name is Jasper."

"Hey, Jasper, I'm Susie."

"I think I overheard you talking to Ms. Daniels about a girl named Lynn."

"Yeah, I did."

"Do you know her last name? Maybe I can answer your question."

"No, I don't. That's why I just have to wait." I take a deep breath, then sigh. "Are you going to the dance by chance?" Jasper asks.

"Maybe! Are you, Jasper?"

"Of course! Hope I'll see you there."

"Everyone in a single-file line, come in, and those who have lunch, go to lunch. Everyone else, proceed to your classes."

I'm actually not hungry.

There are five more minutes of lunch, and finally, the next class. As I head into the classroom, I spot Jasper. It's weird that I hadn't noticed him until now. I'm glad I have. We make eye contact. He smiles, and of course, I smile back. Thirty minutes into class, Principal Leonard dismisses classes for the rest of the day. Oh, okay.

Leaving early, no matter if it's an hour or fifteen minutes. I'm on my way home, walking, enjoying the weather, hoping it doesn't rain today. Swimming is on my to-do list.

When I get home, Mom's not in the kitchen or the living room. Hmmm.

"Mom!" I yell out to see where she could be.
Nothing.

I run upstairs, put my bag in the room, and go past her room. Nope, not in there. I head back downstairs and look out back, and see her relaxing, getting some sun.

"Hey, Mom, having fun?"

"Oh, honey, when did you get here?"

"School let out early today. I've only been here five minutes or so. Is it okay to swim now?"

"Yes, it is."

"I'll be right back."

I dash out the back door and sprint to jump in the pool. "Yahoo!" I make the biggest splash ever. Hehe. This feels amazing. Mom jumps in with me too. After thirty minutes, Mom gets out to head in and start dinner. I stay out for a while. Suddenly I hear my name. But my mom's inside. Who could be calling me? It is not Lynn either. Okay. I hop out of the pool, not getting any answer yet, just looking around.

"Up here, Susie."

"Huh? Hey, I didn't know you live there. I didn't know anyone moved into this house."

"Guess we are supposed to be friends."

"Seems to look that way."

"Hold on, let me come down, okay?"

"All right!"

I walk over to the fence once he gets to his back door.

"How's the water?"

"It's nice. Plus, the rain yesterday made it a little humid out today."

"Yeah, you can say that for sure."

"If you want, you can come swim. That's if you're not busy or have other plans."

He giggles, saying, "I can always fit you into my schedule."

I smile, saying, "Yeah, okay."

He tells me to step back, then hops over the fence. He's showing off, if you ask me, but it's very cute. He runs toward the pool and jumps. In mid-air, knees to chest, he yells, "Haha! "CANNONBALL!"

There's nothing like having fun when your mind needs a break from worrying.

"Susie!" Mom yells as I'm about to dive in.

"Yes, Mama!"

"Oh, didn't know you had company."

As I swim back up to the top fast before mom embarrasses me, and I hear, "Hi, ma'am!"

As I reach the top, I think, *Oh my gosh, how much have I missed? Yikes.*

"Well, hey there, ma'am. Nice to meet you. My name is Jasper. Susie and I go to school together."

"Well, all right, I will leave you both alone. Have fun," she says, smiling while walking back inside the house.

"We are officially friends now. I've met your mom already. Now to meet your father."

"Good luck with that," I say with a sarcastic voice.

"Oh, I'm sorry. Guess I overstepped my boundary."

"Not really. It's just a situation that I don't want to go into."

"Hey, it's cool, no worries. Let's just finish having fun like your mom said."

Hours pass by quickly. To be honest, I don't want the day to end. I know we both have to go inside to eat dinner, but I would like to stay outside.

Laughing, I tell him, "See you tomorrow, Jasper."

"Okay, see ya. Oh, Susie!"

"Yeah, what's up?"

"You can call me Jay Jay if you like."

"Oh, okay, sure. I don't really have a nickname."

"Oh, I'm sure your mom has a sweet nickname for you."

"Wouldn't you want to know?"

We both laugh as we walk toward our back doors.

As I go inside, I catch my mom just smiling.

"So you decided to join me for dinner, my little Susie Q?"

"Of course!" I laugh out loud.

5

"Are you going to tell me about your new friend?"

"Mom, there's not much to say because we just met today. It was pure luck that he lives behind our house. If anything ever comes of it, Mom, you'd be the first to know."

"Okay, honey!"

After doing the dishes and cleaning up the kitchen, I say good night to Mom and head off to bed. Crazy how he has me smiling like this. My cheeks hurt already. Hopefully, I can sleep. After some tossing and turning, trying to get my mind clear, I finally drift off to sleep.

It seems like morning came so quickly. Leaving for school, I try not to get my hopes up about seeing Lynn today because it's so stressful, though in the back of my mind, I really want her to be there today.

The next two days drag by. Still no Lynn. It's just a waiting game now because I don't see her as a friend who would just vanish without telling or saying anything to me. It's now Thursday, and I have to decide whether to go to the dance or not. I'm confused about it all. Lynn wanted me to go so badly, and then she just doesn't come back to school or my house. Jasper wants me to go, but I just don't know him that well. Why make a promise if you're not going to keep it? I'm trying not to get mad over this situation because I know things can happen.

The time has come, and I see Jasper. He comes over to my desk to ask if I have made up my mind about the dance. I explain to him all of what Lynn and I talked about—our plans on going, among other things. He looks me in the eye and begins to say something, but the bell rings. The teacher tells him to get to his seat.

With a small laugh, he smiles, looking up at the teacher, and says, "I'm going, teach. I'm going." He shakes his head as he walks to his seat.

Class is over now. I get up and go out the door.

"Hey, Susie!"

"Yes!"

"Wait up for me."

We walk to lunch, talking. I go to the table I usually sit at, and he comes with me to sit down as well.

I ask, "So you're eating with me today?"

"Yeah! I want to finish asking you what I was going to ask in class before I had to go to my seat."

"Oh, okay. Go ahead."

"Since you haven't heard from your bestie in almost two weeks, how about you go to the dance with me tomorrow?"

"Huh? Let me think about it, okay?"

As he is about to say okay, I interrupt him, saying, "*Absolutely, I will!*"

He has the biggest smile on his face. He gets up, pulls me up from my seat, and hugs me tightly, saying, "You won't regret it."

Lunch is over, and we walk down the hall.

"I have to stop by my locker, okay?"

"Sure."

We walk up to my locker.

He looks at it, saying, "This was the locker of a girl who went missing a year ago. Nobody knew or ever found out what happened to her."

"Wow, really? That sucks."

"Yeah, it does. I guess when you see that her locker has been given away, it's really real. She's not coming back."

Hearing the warning bell ring, we realize that we have to get going. Conversation cut short, we hurry off to class.

"See ya."

"Okay, see ya later."

All right, I have to see if I can get a refund on one of these tickets I got because at this point, I just think something happened in her family. They had to leave or something. I'm going to let myself finally come to accept that she is not able to come.

To the office I go before heading home.

"Hello, Ms. Kim!"

"Hi, Susan! What can I help you with?"

"Well, I was wondering if I can return this ticket."

"Your not going anymore?"

"Oh no! I bought two tickets but I am not sure my friend can go now."

"Okay, well, here. Let me get the envelope for the dance. Here you are. Have a good day."

"Thanks, you as well."

As I head home, I think about how to do my hair for the dance tomorrow. My mom is going to love this. She suspects that something is going on. It's true; moms know everything. I giggle as I hurry through the door.

"Mom!" I yell.

"Yes, honey?" she says as she runs into the living room to make sure all is okay.

"So I got asked to the dance."

"Let me guess… *Jasper*, is it?"

"Yes, Mama!"

"Well, what about Lynn?"

"Still haven't heard from her, so I just returned the ticket."

"Sorry, honey."

"It's really okay, Mom. I think her doing this may be more of a family problem than a me problem, you know."

"Yeah! So how are you thinking of doing your hair?"

"I don't know yet, honestly! Maybe you can help me come up with something pretty."

"Always, my little Susie Q."

There's a sudden knock on the door. Mom and I look at each other.

"You expecting anyone, sweetie?"

"Not that I know of… Oh my gosh, wait a minute. Could it be Lynn?" I shout loudly, running to the door. I open the door with the biggest smile on my face, ready to squeeze her so tightly, then I see Jasper.

He looks at me, saying, "Didn't know you'd be this happy to see me."

Laughing, I step outside to see why the surprise visit. Could he be backing out on me too? Sheesh!

"Oh no, why such a worried look on your face now, Susie? You opened the door with such happiness."

"I was, and I still am, happy. One reason the look turned to kind of a distressed look is that I thought you were Lynn. The second reason is, well, if you just popped up, could this be a cancellation of our plans for the dance? Just overthinking, that's all."

"Okay, well, as you can see, I'm definitely not Lynn. And I'm here to bring news, but it's not anything bad." He then proceeds to let me know that the school forgot to send out newsletters on what they have planned as a special moment. They also didn't announce it before school started or ended.

"Oh, good! So we will not have school tomorrow. The dance will start around 3:30 p.m. My mom and I will pick you up around 2:45 p.m. if that's okay. Normally, I pick a spot to take my date so we can grab something to eat. Can't have you dancing on an empty stomach, you know."

"Oh wow, I'm super excited. I can't wait, actually. Also, what you have planned sounds great. Plus, the time is perfect."

"Well, all right, then. Sounds like a plan." He starts to walk away after discussing everything with me. "Oh hey!"

"Yeah, Jasper?"

"What color dress will you be wearing?"

"It's mint green."

"Oh, perfect, thanks."

"No problem."

"See ya!"

"See ya, Jasper!"

Turning around to open the door, I bump into something. Giggling, I say, "Mom, is that you?"

She steps out from behind the door, holding her head and laughing. "Honey, you almost took me out."

"Sure I did, haha."

I let my mom know the rundown on all that is to happen tomorrow and that I don't have school. "They are doing something new this year for the dance."

"Did he say what it could be?"

"No, I don't really think he knows either."

"Hmmm, interesting. Are you excited?"

"I actually am, Mom. To be honest, it's like a new journey in my life. Also, it's my first date." I start giggling. "That makes it a very special moment in my high school life as a freshman."

Trying on my dress and heels so I can look in the mirror to get an idea of what style would look best, I call out, "Mom!"

"Here I come, honey." She walks into my room, and the look on her face says speechless. She starts crying. "Oh, honey, you look absolutely gorgeous."

"Thanks, Mom."

She reaches for a piece of tissue so she can dry her tears. Now we start doing a few updos. Cute, but we haven't found the perfect one yet. Mom goes out of the room and comes back with the curling iron.

While we wait for it to heat up, she says, "I've got the perfect style for you, honey."

"Okay, Mom, great."

She unplugs the curling iron, stating that I have to trust her and that we will do the hairstyle tomorrow.

"What! Mom, really? You're going to make me wait that long?"

"Time will fly by. Don't you worry your little mind."

I guess she forgot who I am. Laughing to myself, I think, *I am the biggest worrywart of all.*

I put everything back where I need it to be in the morning. I'm glad I embrace my natural beauty. I don't wear makeup; it's too much of a hassle. Also, makeup doesn't allow you to have that natural glow that illuminates your skin in the sunlight.

The alarm clock buzzes so loudly. I try hitting Snooze, but it seems my button is not working this morning. Let me just get up. The room door swings open, and there stands Mom, yelling as loud as she possibly can, "RISE AND SHINE, MY SWEET QUEEN!"

"Really, Mom?" I say as I pull my head from underneath my blanket.

"Come on, honey, let the day begin."

I look over at Kit. "Did you have anything to do with this, hmmm?"

Kit jumps on the bed, meowing at me. She tells me she did.

CHAPTER

After getting up, I take my shower, preparing for this amazing day. Done with that now, I decide if breakfast would be a good idea this morning. No, probably not, because time flies when things are planned. Having a schedule to follow makes you feel rushed.

I go to see if Mom wants to do my hair first or if I should get dressed. As I walk into the living room, it's as if she already knows what I am going to say.

"Nope, sweetie, it will be done after you get ready."

"You sure do know me too well, Mama."

"I do indeed, my lovely daughter."

I walk into the kitchen for a drink of orange juice, trying to sneak a peek out the window to see if I can spot you-know-who. Maybe I can see what he is going to wear. Of course, he has his window blinds closed. Shaking my head and laughing, I go back upstairs.

Entering my room, I walk to my mirror. Sometimes I like to talk to myself in the mirror to play out how I will respond to questions, seeing how cute each facial expression will look. It's not a conceited gesture at all. I just want to make sure I'm cute, adorable, and breathtaking. I cannot be the only one to do so, can I? Now I'm just overthinking.

Looking over at the clock, I say, "Oh, shoot, it's already noon, no way." I start to get dressed, constantly looking into the mirror like, "Does this look right? No. Maybe put it this way." Finally, I just take a deep breath, saying to myself, "Everything is okay. Just relax." Cool, calm, and relaxed, now I can finish.

Done, I head to my mom for the finishing touches. I glance at the clock before leaving my room. It's 1:30 p.m. With an hour and fifteen minutes left, I'm so ready. My mom yells for me to come into her room. I walk in, and she has set up the cutest spot for me to sit at. But one thing is missing.

"Mom!"

"Yes, sweetheart?"

"Where is the mirror?"

"Oh, you don't need that."

"How will I know if I am going to like it?"

"You won't until I'm all done."

"Oh, you're really trying to give me a heart attack, Mama."

Giggling, she says, "Not at all. Come on now, honey."

As I get seated, she puts a sheet over me so nothing can get on my dress.

"Mom, you've really got me feeling like a queen, that's for sure."

Smiling, she begins.

It's about 2:20 p.m.

"All done, honey. Go take a look."

I can't run in the heels I have on, so I walk patiently down the hall to the bathroom. Before clicking on the light, I drift into a memory of when my dad said, "Sue darling, I just can't wait until I get to see you at your first prom. Your mom will be nice to your date. I will have to scare them so they know not to hurt my sweet babe." Then I snap out of it when I hear a knock on the door. Oh no, I haven't looked at myself yet.

"Susie, honey, the door is for you."

Shoot!

I start walking down the stairs. Jasper, his mom, and my mom all look up at me. His mom nudges him, saying, "She is absolutely gorgeous."

He smiles, whispering back to her, "Oh, how I do know so."

As I reach the last step, he reaches for my hand to help me down, then puts my corsage on me. He tells me, "You look amazingly beautiful."

"Thanks," I say, and I let him know he looks handsome.

Our moms are so excited; all we see are flashes from their cameras. No warning, no "Get ready to pose," just taking pictures and videos.

We both laugh it off, then start striking poses for them. Already everything is going well.

"Ready to head off, you both?"

"Yes! Mom, I will see you later."

"Okay, my Susie Q. Have fun, you both."

"Yes, ma'am, we definitely will."

As we walk to the car, he opens my door.

"Such a gentleman I see."

He fixes his collar, saying, "I do have manners, you know." He gets in the back seat with me. I think that's super sweet. As we are driving off, he smiles, saying, "I figured out your nickname."

"Oh gosh! No! No! No, you don't." Giggling, I feel myself getting hot. "May I crack the window?"

His mom says, "Of course."

We arrive at the restaurant, which is super fancy. I didn't really expect this kind of fine dining. Going in, the waitress greets us.

"Jasper Johnson?" she says.

"Yes, ma'am."

"Follow me."

As we are seated at our table, I am very amazed at how he did all of this just for me. *Way to treat a lady,* I think.

After finishing our meal, his mom comes in to let us know it's about 3:15 p.m. We have fifteen minutes to get to the dance. As we exit the restaurant and get back in the car, he leans over, saying, "Thank you."

"Why?"

"For being such an amazing person who took the time out of their day to make a special memory with me."

Wow! I think I just met my Prince Charming.

When we get to the dance, he opens the door for me once again.

His mom asks, "What time should I come back?"

He looks at me, asking, "Do you plan on staying the whole night, or should we leave in about an hour or two?"

"Let's plan to stay the whole time."

"You heard her, Mom."

"Okay, you both enjoy yourselves."

At the entrance to the dance, all of his friends and their dates are waiting for us. We head that way. I look around for Lynn just to see if maybe she would pop up as a surprise or something. Not at all.

Jasper introduces me to everyone. I start to realize it.

"Oh my gosh, Jasper, you're the quarterback of the football team?"

"Well, yeah," he says, laughing.

"You didn't tell me that part."

"I would have eventually. I didn't want you to run away. I wanted you to get to know me for me, not for being the popular jock at school."

Giggling, I say, "Yeah, you do have a point."

It's so beautifully decorated in here. I love the theme and colors. Everyone is dancing and having fun. Then Principal Leonard gets up on the stage. He grabs the microphone and asks for the DJ to turn the music off for a moment.

"How is everyone doing tonight?"

We all start clapping, yelling, screaming, and cheering!

"Okay, great. Now I would like to say a few words about this specific dance and prom theme. As you all know, last year we had a student who suddenly disappeared."

"Jasper," I say, "is this the girl you were talking about?"

"Yes, Susie, it is."

"We want to do something to let everyone know she is not forgotten. We will forever remember her."

Suddenly a large poster comes down. On this poster is a girl wearing a cheerleader uniform. As the spotlight moves toward it and lights it up, my face goes pale. Everyone is cheering and clapping. I turn to the door and begin to run as fast as I can. Jasper yells for me, but I don't stop. I keep going. From outside, I hear them all chanting her name, Lynn. I can't believe this. How could that be? I kick my heels off. While I run down the road, rain starts to pour down. A car drives by fast, swerving. I think they may have lost control. I jump out of the way, tumbling down this steep hill into some kind of creek. Yuck!

I get up to walk again, then I trip over something. It looks to be a shoe or something. As I make sure I have my heels, lightning lights up the sky. That's when I notice the Best Friend charm like mine. I take off running even faster, crying.

"Why! Why would Lynn throw it down here? Promises, huh? Never trust a promise," I say as I make it to my front door.

Before I open it, Lynn comes from the side of the bush.

"Sorry I'm late, Susie. A lot has been going on with me lately."

"Are you serious, Lynn? It's been two whole weeks without hearing from you. Also, I found where you threw our Best Friend charm."

"Wait, what? It's right—" She goes to feel for it. "It's not there. No, Susie, I don't think you understand. The day we left school, I went home. I've been trying to talk to my mom, but she hasn't been listening to me. It's like I don't exist to her anymore since my dad left a year ago."

"Wait! Your dad left a year ago?"

"Yes! I got mad because she wouldn't give me an answer about whether she would take us or take me to pick out a dress."

Everything starts adding up to me. I look at Lynn. "Lynn," I say, "I think, well, how do I say this… I think you're dead."

As I say that, a loud boom echoes in the sky, lighting it up. We look at each other in shock. Jasper runs up my driveway, and my mom opens the door.

"What's going on, Susie? Who are you talking to?"

Jasper makes it to the door. "Why did you leave like that?"

So many questions are coming to me. I look at everyone and ask, "You don't see her?"

Kit pokes her head out and rubs against me with that sweet purr. No one answers me. Lynn just runs off in disbelief.

My mom says, "Have you been drinking?"

Jasper's face has "lost and confused" written all over it.

"You both get inside now. Susie, you have some explaining to do. Would you like me to call your mom, Jasper, or would you like to?"

He stands in the living room, still confused about everything.

"Mom, he has nothing to do with this situation, seriously."

"Actually, ma'am, I will call my mom to have her come over. It's understandable how it may seem to you, finding Susie all muddy and shoeless. She definitely didn't leave this way earlier."

"Mom, listen, I ran off from the dance."

"What! Why would you do that, honey?"

"Well, I've told you about Lynn, how she just disappeared or stopped being my friend, I guess."

"Yeah, I do remember how upset you had been because you hadn't heard from her."

A knock on the door brings the conversation to a stop.

Jasper says, "I think that's my mom."

"I'm gonna get the door," my mom says.

Jasper has a soft smile on his face. "You didn't have to run off like that, you know."

"I just got overwhelmed. How do I explain to my date that the cheerleader on the poster is my friend Lynn, who just left without any notice? Then I find out she's dead. It's a bit awkward, you know."

He giggles and says, "That's understandable. Can I tell you something, though?"

"Sure!"

"No matter what it may be, if you ever are going through something, I want to be who you can come talk to. You know, someone you tell all your problems to."

"Really, Jasper?"

"Yes, really! I promise, Susie."

"Jasper," we hear in a serious voice.

"Mom!"

"What is going on?"

"Just tonight, at the dance, they did a memorial in memory of Lynn."

"Oh, Jas, are you okay?"

Huh? I think. *Why did she ask him that?*

"Yeah, Mom, I'm okay. That's not what had me leave. It was Susie running out of there so quickly."

"Oh my, Susie, did you know her as well, dear?"

"Not necessarily."

That's when Jasper chimes in, "Well, that's why I called you over, Mom."

"Would anyone like something to drink?" Mom says.

"No, thank you!" everyone replies.

Where do I start?

Jasper starts to talk about how much Lynn was loved at school. She always kept a smile on her face, was fun to be around, and had a very caring heart.

"That's why I was shocked the school had given you her locker. She had a friend that lived in the house, actually. Emily was her name. When Lynn went missing, Emily couldn't bear the thought of her best friend out there all alone. Nevertheless, search parties looked for her. Nothing, not a trace of Lynn. Every day, Emily came to school but wasn't her normal self. Eventually, she stopped going to school. Her parents sold the house, then you guys moved in.

I start thinking about how Lynn could be feeling now.

Back at Lynn's house, she is in her room. All she can do is cry while looking at all the memories of her with all her friends. "Could this all be true? If so, how did Susie see and hear me?"

Lynn hears her mom come into her room; she opens the door and walks to the bed to sit down.

"Oh, my sweet Lynn, it's been a year since you left. If only I knew what happened. If you're okay… If…if… Oh gosh, all these ifs."

Seeing her mom like this truly hurts her. But what can she do if she just doesn't see Lynn? Lynn walks around the room to try to move something or knock something over, and a picture falls off the wall. It's of Jasper and her.

Lynn's mom looks quickly. She gets up to pick it up. She stares at it for a while, then says, "If your dad had just let you go to the dance with him that night…"

Knock, knock, knock!

Who could be at the door at this time of night?

"Who is it?"

"It's Jasper!"

"What? I mean, why are you here?"

Opening the door, Lynn's mom say, "Hello, Jasper. What may I help you with?"

"Well, first, let me introduce you to Susie."

"Hi!"

"Well, hello."

"We've come by because Susie may know where Lynn could be."

"What! Now, wait just a second. What kind of sick joke are you playing here?"

"No, please, just hear me out. I understand that you don't know me. I'm not going to drag this out with a long story, so I will just get right to it. I moved here a few months ago. Tonight the school did a remembrance for your daughter. When I saw the poster of her, she looked really familiar. Getting overwhelmed, I ran out of prom, which led to me falling down a hill because of a car losing control in the rain. To avoid getting hit, I jumped out of the way and tumbled down the hill into a creek area. It was dark and rainy, but I tripped over a shoe, which made me stop. I had to check if I still had my heels in my hand. That's when the lightning lit up the sky. This Best Friend charm was given to me by a girl named Lynn, who actually looks just like your daughter. The matching charm necklace was there by the shoe."

"Huh? So are you saying my daughter, who has been missing for a year, gave you that charm?"

"It sounds crazy, but yes, ma'am, that's what I'm saying. Can you call the police now? And let's get there before the rain washes it down the creek bed."

"Okay! Let me think. What you kids have told me is a lot to take in."

We all hear glass shattering.

"No one is here. What could that be? How could that have fallen out of nowhere? Maybe that's

Lynn telling me to trust what you are saying. Shoot! Come on, kids, take me there."

We drive to the place where I saw it, and when we get there, we go down the hill. Lynn's mom stops abruptly, knees hitting the ground, crying hysterically. Jasper puts his head down, trying not to let me see his tears fall.

She calls the police to give the location, then calls Lynn's dad, which seems very hard for her to do. As soon as he answers, she starts to apologize for putting him through all of what he was trying to heal and be strong.

He stops her, saying, "Tell me where to go."

She lets him know.

"I'm on my way," he says.

Getting off the phone, she looks over to us. "Thank you both for bringing us peace for what we've never been able to get over."

"You are welcome," we both say.

"Do you kids need a ride home?"

"No, ma'am! Thanks, though. We would like to stay until someone gets here and stays with you."

Right as we say that, police lights, sirens, and cars pull up. So does Lynn's dad. He runs to her and hugs her, apologizing for everything. Officers ask questions. She points to the place where Lynn's belongings are on the ground. We start to walk away.

Lynn's dad says loudly, "Hey."

We stop and turn around to look in his direction.

He comes up to Jasper, apologizes to him for everything he put him through because he was dating his daughter.

Jasper, of course, accepts the apology. He then looks over to me, telling me I was their angel sent to bring them peace, and he thanks me for not being afraid to let her mom know what I discovered.

We leave and make it home safe.

Jasper walks me up to my door. "Today was definitely a day that we will not forget, huh?"

"Right!"

"Can I ask you something?"

"Sure, Jasper, ask away."

"Will you consider being my girlfriend?"

"What? Really?"

"Don't answer that."

"Yes, yes, yes! I will be your girlfriend."

He smiles and says, "Good night."

"Good night," I say, smiling back at him.

"See you tomorrow, my Susie Q."

I shake my head, giggling as I go through the door. He got that one off, but man, I'll get him back later.

Going inside the house, Mom asks, "Susie, honey, how did it go?"

"Lynn's mom took it as a joke. She was very upset, thinking we were playing a cruel joke on her. Some glass or something fell in the middle of us talking with her. I guess she took it as a sign from Lynn because after hearing it shatter, we got into the car and went to the spot where it all happened."

"Well, I am glad you were brave enough to do such a thing."

"Yeah, Mom, me too."

"How's Jasper doing?"

"He's better now. Lynn's dad apologized to him tonight."

"Wow, that's amazing."

"Yes, it takes too much energy hating someone, as well as holding a grudge, you know."

"Susie, you are just so sweet and kind."

"I'd like to think I get it from you, Mom."

"How are you feeling, knowing all of this about Lynn?"

"If all of this had to happen to help others heal, I'm truly okay with it. Does it hurt? Yes. Will I think of her? Yes. But looking at the positive side of it, Lynn's parents have closure now." Then I add, "I'm Jasper's girlfriend," smiling big.

"Oh really, huh?"

"Indeed, Mama."

We both laugh.

"One thing I've learned is to never make a promise."

"Why is that, Susie, sweetheart?"

"We may never know what tomorrow may bring. You can't promise something you have no control over what fate has intended."

About the Author

Latoya, known to most people as Toya, is from Missouri, where she was born and raised. Since she was a kid, her imagination has been out of this world. She can tell stories, making whoever is listening or reading feel like they are living it. It's a gift to be able to reach people with words, giving them this rush of "What will happen next?" or just not being able to stop listening or reading, keeping their attention with the biggest smile on their face. She likes to keep people interested in her stories as it unfolds. Overall, she's just herself.